Gabriel and the Hour Book

BY Evaleen Stein

Originally published in 1906.

TO

My friend

CAROLINE H. GRIFFITHS

CONTENTS

CHAPTER I.

THE LITTLE COLOUR GRINDER

IT was a bright morning of early April, many hundred years ago; and through all the fields and meadows of Normandy the violets and cuckoo-buds were just beginning to peep through the tender green of the young grass. The rows of tall poplar-trees that everywhere, instead of fences, served to mark off the farms of the country folk, waved in the spring wind like great, pale green plumes; and among their branches the earliest robins and field-fares were gaily singing as a little boy stepped out from a small thatched cottage standing among the fields, and took his way along the highroad.

That Gabriel Viaud was a peasant lad, any one could have told from the blouse of blue homespun, and the wooden shoes which he wore; and that he felt the gladness of the April time could easily be known by the happy little song he began to sing to himself, and by the eager delight with which he now and then stooped to pluck a blue violet or to gather a handful of golden cuckoo-buds.

A mile or two behind him, and hidden by a bend in the road, lay the little village of St. Martin-de-Bouchage; while in the soft blue distance ahead of him rose the gray walls of St. Martin's Abbey, whither he was going.

Indeed, for almost a year now the little boy had been trudging every day to the Abbey, where he earned a small sum by waiting upon the good brothers who dwelt there, and who made the beautiful painted books for which the Abbey had become famous. Gabriel could grind and mix their colours for them, and prepare the parchment on which they did their writing, and could do many other little things that helped them in their work.

The lad enjoyed his tasks at the Abbey, and, above all, delighted in seeing the beautiful things at which the brothers were always busy; yet, as he now drew near the gateway, he could not help but give a little sigh, for it was so bright and sunny out-of-doors. He smiled, though, as he looked at the gay bunches of blossoms with which he had quite filled his hands, and felt that at least he was taking a bit of the April in with him, as he crossed the threshold and entered a large room.

"Good morrow, Gabriel," called out several voices as he came in, for the lad was a general favourite with the brothers; and Gabriel, respectfully taking off his blue peasant cap, gave a pleasant "good morrow" to each.

The room in which he stood had plain stone walls and a floor of paved stone, and little furniture, except a number of solidly made benches and tables. These were placed beneath a row of high windows, and the tables were covered with writing and painting materials and pieces of parchment; for the brotherhood of St. Martin's was very industrious.

In those days,--it was four hundred years ago,--

printed books were very few, and almost unknown to most people; for printing-presses had been invented only a few years, and so by far the greater number of books in the world were still made by the patient labour of skilful hands; the work usually being done by the monks, of whom there were very many at that time.

These monks, or brothers, as they were often called, lived in monasteries and abbeys, and were men who banded themselves together in brotherhoods, taking solemn vows never to have homes of their own or to mingle in the daily life of others, but to devote their lives to religion; for they believed that they could serve God better by thus shutting themselves off from the world.

And so it came about that the brothers, having more time and more learning than most other people of those days, made it their chief work to preserve and multiply all the books that were worth keeping. These they wrote out on parchment (for paper was very scarce so long ago), and then ornamented the pages with such beautiful painted borders of flowers and birds and saints and angels, and such lovely initial letters, all in bright colours and gold, that to this day large numbers of the beautiful books made by the monks are still kept among the choicest treasures of the museums and great libraries of the world.

And few of all those wonderful old illuminations (for so the painted ornaments were called) were lovelier than the work of the brotherhood of St. Martin's. Gabriel felt very proud even to grind the

colours for them. But as he passed over to one of
the tables and began to make ready his paint mortar,
the monk who had charge of the writing-room
called to him, saying:

"Gabriel, do not get out thy work here, for the
Abbot hath just ordered that some one must help
Brother Stephen, who is alone in the old chapter-
house. He hath a special book to make, and his
colour-grinder is fallen ill; so go thou at once and
take Jacques's place."

So Gabriel left the writing-room and passed down
the long corridor that led to the chapter-house. This
was a room the brothers had kept for years as a
meeting-place, when they and the Abbot, who
governed them all, wished to talk over the affairs of
the Abbey; but as it had at last grown too small for
them, they had built a new and larger one; and so
the old chapter-house was seldom used any more.

Gabriel knew this, and he wondered much why
Brother Stephen chose to work there rather than in
the regular writing-room with the others. He
supposed, however, that, for some reason of his
own, Brother Stephen preferred to be alone.

He did not know that the monk, at that moment, was
sitting moodily by his work-table, his eyes staring
aimlessly ahead of him, and his hands dropped idly
in his lap. For Brother Stephen was feeling very
cross and unhappy and out of sorts with all the
world. And this was the reason: poor Brother
Stephen had entered the Abbey when a lad scarcely
older than Gabriel. He had come of good family,

but had been left an orphan with no one to care for him, and for want of other home had been sent to the Abbey, to be trained for the brotherhood; for in those days there were few places where fatherless and motherless children could be taken care of.

As little Jean (for this was his name before he joined the monks, when one's own name was always changed) grew up, he took the solemn vows which bound him to the rules of the brotherhood without realizing what it all would mean to him; for Brother Stephen was a born artist; and, by and by, he began to feel that while life in the Abbey was well for most of the brothers, for him it was not well. He wanted to be free to wander about the world; to paint pictures of many things; and to go from city to city, and see and study the work of the world's great artists.

It is true he spent the greater part of his time in the Abbey working on the illuminated books, and this he loved; yet it did not wholly satisfy him. He longed to paint other things, and, above all, his artist nature longed for freedom from all the little rules of daily life that governed the days of the brotherhood.

Brother Stephen had brooded much over this desire for freedom, and only the day before had sought out the Abbot of St. Martin's and asked to be released from the vows of obedience which he had taken years before, but which now he found so hard to live up to. But, to his great disappointment, the Abbot had refused to grant his request.

The Abbot had several reasons for this refusal; one of them was that he himself dearly loved all the little daily ceremonies of the Abbey, and he could not understand why any one who had once lived there could prefer a life in the world. He really thought it was for Brother Stephen's own good that he should stay in the brotherhood.

And then, too, perhaps there was another reason less to the Abbot's credit; and this reason was that of all the beautiful illuminated books for which the Abbey of St. Martin's had become so famous, none were quite so exquisitely done as those made by Brother Stephen. So perhaps the Abbot did not wish to lose so skilful an artist from the work-room of the Abbey, and especially at this particular time. For just before Brother Stephen had had his talk with the Abbot, a messenger from the city of Paris had come to the Abbey, bearing an order from the king, Louis XII., who reigned over France, and Normandy also, which was a part of France.

Now the following winter, the king was to wed the Lady Anne of Bretagne; and as Lady Anne was a great admirer and collector of beautiful painted books, the king thought no gift would please his bride quite so much as a piece of fine illumination; and he decided that it should be an hour book. These books were so called because in them were written different parts of the Bible, intended to be read at certain hours of the day; for most people at that time were very devout, and the great ladies especially were very fond of having their hour books made as beautiful as possible.

As King Louis thought over the best places where he might have his bride's gift painted, at last he made up his mind to send to the monks of St. Martin's. He commanded that the hour book be done in the most beautiful style, and that it must be finished by the following December.

The Abbot was delighted with the honour the king had shown the Abbey in sending this order; and he determined that Brother Stephen should stay and make the entire book, as no one else wrote so evenly, or made quite such lovely initials and borders as did he.

When the Abbot told this to Brother Stephen, however, it was a pity that he did so in such a cold and haughty way that altogether Brother Stephen's anger was aroused, for he had a rather unruly temper; and so, smarting under the disappointment of not receiving his liberty, and feeling that the book for Lady Anne was one cause of this, he had spoken angrily and disrespectfully to the Abbot, and refused point-blank to touch the king's order.

At this the Abbot in his turn became angry, and declared that Brother Stephen should be compelled to paint the hour book whether he wished to or not; that he must do it as punishment for his unruly conduct; and the Abbot threatened, moreover, that if he did not obey, he would be placed under the ban of the Church, which was considered by all the brotherhood as a dreadful misfortune.

And so with this threat hanging over him, that very morning, just before Gabriel reached the Abbey,

Brother Stephen had been sent to the old chapter-house, where he was ordered to work by himself, and to begin the book at once. And to complete his humiliation, and for fear he might try to run away, the Abbot caused him to be chained to one of the legs of the heavy work-table; and this chain he was to wear every day during working hours.

Now all this made Brother Stephen very angry and unhappy, and his heart was full of bitterness toward the Abbot and all of the brotherhood and the world in general, when all at once he heard Gabriel's knock at the door; and then, in another moment, the door was softly pushed open, and there, on the threshold, stood the little boy.

CHAPTER II.

BROTHER STEPHEN'S INSPIRATION

GABRIEL knew nothing of Brother Stephen's troubles, and so was smiling happily as he stepped into the room, holding his cap in one hand, while with his other arm he hugged to him his large bunch of violets and cuckoo-buds. Indeed he looked so bright and full of life that even Brother Stephen felt the effect of it, and his frown began to smooth out a little as he said:

"Well, my lad, who art thou?"

"I am Gabriel Viaud, Brother Stephen," answered

the boy, "and I have come to help you; for they told me Jacques is fallen ill. What would you like me to do first?"

To this Brother Stephen scarcely knew what to reply. He was certainly in no mood for work. He was still very, very angry, and thought himself terribly misused by the Abbot; and though he greatly dreaded the latter's threats, he had almost reached the point of defying him and the king and everybody else, no matter what dreadful thing happened to him afterward.

But then as he looked again at the bright-faced little boy standing there, and seeming so eager to help, he began to relent more and more; and besides, he found it decidedly embarrassing to try to explain things to Gabriel.

So after a little pause, he said to him: "Gabriel, I am not ready for thee at this moment; go sit on yonder bench. I wish to think out a matter which is perplexing me." Then as Gabriel obediently went over to the bench and seated himself, he added: "Thou canst pass the time looking at the books on the shelf above thee."

So while Brother Stephen was trying to make up his mind as to what he would do, Gabriel took down one of the books, and was soon absorbed in its pages. Presently, as he turned a new one, he gave a little involuntary exclamation of delight. At this Brother Stephen noticed him, and--

"Ah!" he said, "what hast thou found that seems to

please thee?"

"Oh, sir," answered Gabriel, "this is the most
beautiful initial letter I have ever seen!"

Now Gabriel did not know that the book had been
made a few years before by Brother Stephen
himself, and so he had no idea how much it pleased
the brother to have his work admired.

Indeed, most people who do good work of any kind
oftentimes feel the need of praise; not flattery, but
the real approval of some one who understands
what they are trying to do. It makes the workman or
artist feel that if his work is liked by somebody, it is
worth while to try to do more and better.

Poor Brother Stephen did not get much of this
needed praise, for many of the other monks at the
Abbey were envious of him, and so were unwilling
really to admire his work; while the Abbot was so
cold and haughty and so taken up with his own
affairs, that he seldom took the trouble to say what
he liked or disliked.

So when Brother Stephen saw Gabriel's eager
admiration, he felt pleased indeed; for Gabriel had a
nice taste in artistic things, and seemed instinctively
to pick out the best points of anything he looked at.
And when, in his enthusiasm, he carried the book
over and began to tell Brother Stephen why he so
much admired the painting, without knowing it, he
really made the latter feel happier than he had felt
for many a day. He began to have a decided notion
that he would paint King Louis's book after all. And

just then, as if to settle the matter, he happened to glance at the corner of the table where Gabriel had laid down his bunch of flowers as he came in.

It chanced that some of the violets had fallen from the cluster and dropped upon a broad ruler of brass that lay beside the painting materials. And even as Brother Stephen looked, it chanced also that a little white butterfly drifted into the room through the bars of the high, open window; after vaguely fluttering about for a while, at last, attracted by the blossoms, it came, and, poising lightly over the violets on the ruler, began to sip the honey from the heart of one of them.

As Brother Stephen's artistic eye took in the beauty of effect made by the few flowers on the brass ruler with the butterfly hovering over them, he, too, gave a little exclamation, and his eyes brightened and he smiled; for he had just got a new idea for an illuminated border.

"Yes," he said to himself, "this would be different from any I have yet seen! I will decorate King Louis's book with borders of gold; and on the gold I will paint the meadow wildflowers, and the bees and butterflies, and all the little flying creatures."

Now before this, all the borders of the Abbey books had been painted, in the usual manner of the time, with scrolls and birds and flowers more or less conventionalized; that is, the artists did not try to make them look exactly like the real ones, but twisted them about in all sorts of fantastic ways. Sometimes the stem of a flower would end in the curled-up folds of a winged dragon, or a bird would have strange blossoms growing out of his beak, or perhaps the tips of his wings.

These borders were indeed exquisitely beautiful, but Brother Stephen was just tired of it all, and wanted to do something quite different; so he was delighted with his new idea of painting the field-flowers exactly like nature, only placing them on a background of gold.

As he pictured in his mind one page after another thus adorned, he became more and more interested and impatient to begin at once. He forgot all about his anger at the Abbot; he forgot everything else, except that he wanted to begin King Louis's book as quickly as possible!

And so he called briskly to Gabriel, who meantime had reseated himself on his bench:

"Gabriel, come hither! Canst thou rule lines without blotting? Canst thou make ink and grind colours and prepare gold size?"

"Yes, sir," said Gabriel, surprised at the monk's eager manner, "I have worked at all these things."

"Good!" replied Brother Stephen. "Here is a piece of parchment thou canst cut and prepare, and then rule it, thus" (and here he showed him how he wished it done), "with scarlet ink. But do not take yonder brass ruler! Here is one of ivory thou canst use instead."

And then as Gabriel went to work, Brother Stephen, taking a goose-quill pen and some black ink, began skilfully and carefully to make drawings of the violets as they lay on the ruler, not forgetting the white butterfly which still hovered about. The harder he worked the happier he grew; hour after hour passed, till at last the dinner time came, and Gabriel, who was growing very hungry, could hear the footsteps of the brothers, as they marched into the large dining-room where they all ate together.

Brother Stephen, however, was so absorbed that he did not notice anything; till, by and by, the door opened, and in came two monks, one carrying some soup and bread and a flagon of wine. As they entered, Brother Stephen turned quickly, and was about to rise, when all at once he felt the tug of the chain still fastened about the leg of the table; at this his face grew scarlet with shame, and he sank back in his chair.

Gabriel started with surprise, for he had not before seen the chain, partly hidden as it was by the folds of the brother's robe. As he looked, one of the two monks went to the table, and, with a key which he carried, unlocked the chain so Brother Stephen might have a half-hour's liberty while he ate. The monks, however, stayed with him to keep an eye on his movements; and meantime they told Gabriel to go out to the Abbey kitchen and find something for his own dinner.

As Gabriel went out along the corridor to the kitchen, his heart swelled with pity! Why was Brother Stephen chained? He tried to think, and remembered that once before he had seen one of the brothers chained to a table in the writing-room because he was not diligent enough with his work,-- but Brother Stephen! Was he not working so hard? And how beautiful, too, were his drawings! The more Gabriel thought of it the more indignant he grew. Indeed, he did not half-enjoy the bread and savoury soup made of black beans, that the cook dished out for him; he took his wooden bowl, and sitting on a bench, ate absently, thinking all the while of Brother Stephen.

When he had finished he went back to the chapter-house and found the other monks gone and Brother Stephen again chained. Gabriel felt much embarrassed to have been obliged to see it; and when Brother Stephen, pointing to the chain, said bitterly, "Thou seest they were afraid I would run away from my work," the lad was so much at a loss to know what to say, that he very wisely said nothing.

Now Brother Stephen, though he had begun the book as the Abbot wished, yet he had by no means the meek and penitent spirit which also the Abbot desired of him, and which it was proper for a monk to have.

And so if the truth must be told, each time the other monks came in to chain him, he felt more than anything else like seizing both of them, and thrusting them bodily out of the door, or at least trying to do so. But then he could not forget the Abbot's threat if he showed disobedience; and he had been brought up to dread the ban of the Church more than anything else that could possibly happen to him, because he believed that this would make him unhappy, not only in this life, but in the life to come. And so he smothered his feelings and tried to bear the humiliation as patiently as he could.

Gabriel could not help but see, however, that it took him some time to regain the interest he had felt in his work, and it was not until the afternoon was half-gone that he seemed to forget his troubles enough really to have heart in the pages he was making.

When dusk fell, Gabriel picked up and arranged his things in order, and bidding Brother Stephen good night, trudged off home.

CHAPTER III.

GABRIEL INTERVIEWS THE ABBOT

THE next day of Gabriel's service passed off much the same as the first, and so it went for almost a week; but the boy saw day by day that Brother Stephen's chain became more and more unbearable to him, and that he had long fits of brooding, when he looked so miserable and unhappy that Gabriel's heart fairly ached for him.

At last the lad, who was a sympathetic little fellow, felt that he could stand it no longer, but must try and help him in some way.

"If I could only speak to the Abbot himself," thought Gabriel, "surely he would see that Brother Stephen is set free!"

The Abbot, however, was a very stately and dignified person; and Gabriel did not quite see how a little peasant boy like himself could find an opportunity to speak to him, or how he would dare to say anything even if he had a chance.

Now it happened the very morning that Gabriel was thinking about all this, he was out in the Abbey kitchen beating up the white of a nice fresh egg which he had brought with him from home that day. He had the egg in an earthen bowl, and was working away with a curious wooden beater, for few people had forks in those days. And as he beat up the white froth, the Abbey cooks also were very busy making pasties, and roasting huge pieces of meat before the great open fireplace, and baking loaves of sweet Normandy bread for the monks' dinner.

But Gabriel was not helping them; no, he was beating the egg for Brother Stephen to use in putting on the gold in the border he was painting. For the brothers did not have the imitation gold powders of which we see so much to-day; but instead, they used real gold, which they ground up very fine in earthen mortars, and took much trouble to properly prepare. And when they wanted to lay it on, they commonly used the white of a fresh egg to fasten it to the parchment.

So Gabriel was working as fast as he could, for

Brother Stephen was waiting; when all at once he happened to look out the kitchen door, which opened on a courtyard where there was a pretty garden, and he saw the Abbot walking up and down the gravel paths, and now and then stopping to see how the tulips and daffodils were coming on.

As Gabriel looked, the Abbot seated himself on a stone bench; and then the little boy, forgetting his awe of him, and thinking only of Brother Stephen and his chain ran out as fast as he could, still holding his bowl in one hand and the wooden beater in the other.

As he came up to where the Abbot was sitting, he courtesied in such haste that he spilled out half his egg as he eagerly burst out:

"O reverend Father! will you not command Brother Stephen to be set free from his chain?"

The Abbot at first had smiled at the droll figure made by the little boy, whom he supposed to be one of the kitchen scullions, but at this speech he stiffened up and looked very stern as Gabriel went on breathlessly:

"He is making such a beautiful book, and he works so hard; but the chain is so dreadful to him, and I was sure that if you knew they had put it on him, you would not allow it!"

Here the Abbot began to feel a trifle uncomfortable, for he saw that Gabriel did not know that he himself had ordered Brother Stephen to wear the chain. But he mentioned nothing of this as he spoke to Gabriel.

"Boy," he said, severely, "what affair of thine is this matter about Brother Stephen? Doubtless if he is chained, it is a punishment he hath merited. 'Tis scarcely becoming in a lad like thee to question these things." And then, as he looked sharply at Gabriel, he added, "Did Brother Stephen send thee hither? Who art thou?"

At this Gabriel hung his head, and, "Nay, sir," he answered, simply, "he does not know, and perhaps he will be angry with me! I am his colour-grinder, and I was in the kitchen getting the egg for his gold,"--here suddenly Gabriel remembered his bowl, and looking down in dismay, "Oh, sir," he exclaimed, "I have spilled the egg, and it was fresh-laid this morning by my white hen!" Here the boy looked so honestly distressed that the Abbot could not but believe that he spoke the truth, and so he smiled a little as he said, not unkindly:

"Well, never mind about thy hen,--go on; thou wast in the kitchen, and then what?"

"I saw you in the garden," answered Gabriel, "and--and--I thought that if you knew about the chain, you would not like it;" (here the Abbot began to look very stern again); "and," Gabriel added, "I could not bear to see Brother Stephen so unhappy. I know he is unhappy, for whenever he notices the chain, he frowns and his hand trembles so he can hardly paint!"

"Ah," said the Abbot to himself, "if his hand

trembles, that is another matter." For the Abbot knew perfectly well that in order to do successfully anything so delicate as a piece of illumination, one must have a steady hand and untroubled nerves; and he began to think that perhaps he had gone a little too far in punishing Brother Stephen. So he thought a minute, and then to Gabriel, who was still standing before him, not quite knowing what to do, he merely said:

"Go back to thy work, lad, and mind thy colours; and," he added with haughty dignity, "I will do as I think best about Brother Stephen's chain."

So Gabriel went back to the kitchen feeling very uncomfortable, for he was afraid he had displeased the Abbot, and so, perhaps, done more harm than good to Brother Stephen. While he was quite sure he had displeased Brother Stephen, for he had kept him waiting a long while, and worse still, had spilled the best egg there was in the kitchen! However, the lad begged one of the cooks to let him have another egg, and, whisking it up as quickly as he could, made haste to carry it to the chapter-house.

As he pushed open the door, Brother Stephen said, sharply, "How now! I thought they had chained thee to one of the tables of the kitchen!"

"I am so sorry," said Gabriel, his face very red,-- "but--I--I spilled the first egg and had to make ready another."

He hoped Brother Stephen would not ask him how

he happened to spill it; for by this time he began to realize that the high-spirited monk probably had reasons of his own for submitting to the punishment of the chain, and that very likely he would be displeased if he knew that his little colour-grinder had asked the Abbot to free him. So Gabriel felt much relieved when, without further questions, Brother Stephen went on with his work, in which for the moment he was greatly absorbed.

And thus the day went quietly on, till early in the afternoon; when, to the great surprise of both of them, the door slowly opened, and in walked the Abbot himself.

The Abbot was haughty, as usual, and, as Brother Stephen saw him come in, he raised his head with an involuntary look of pride and resentment; but neither spoke as the Abbot stepped over to the table, and examined the page on which the monk was working.

This particular page happened to be ornamented with a wide border of purple flag-flowers, copied from some Gabriel had gathered the day before in a swampy corner of one of the wayside meadows. Their fresh green leaves and rich purple petals shone with royal effect against the background of gold; while hovering over them, and clinging to their stems, were painted honey-bees, with gauzy wings, and soft, furry-looking bodies of black and gold.

As the Abbot saw how beautiful it all was, and how different from any other of the Abbey illuminations, he smiled to himself with pleasure. For the Abbot, though he never said a great deal, yet very well knew a good piece of artistic work when he saw it. Instead of merely smiling to himself, however, it would have made Brother Stephen much happier if he had taken the trouble to say aloud some of the nice things he was thinking about the work.

For Brother Stephen felt very bitter as he thought over all he had been made to bear; and even as the Abbot looked, he saw, sure enough, that his hand trembled as Gabriel had said; for the poor monk had hard work to control his feelings.

Now the Abbot really did not mean to be unkind. It was only that he did not quite know how to unbend; and perhaps feeling this, he soon went out.

Gabriel, who had been very much afraid he might say something to him about their conversation of the morning, felt greatly relieved when the door closed behind him; and the rest of the afternoon he and Brother Stephen worked on in silence.

CHAPTER IV.

THE HOUR BOOK

BUT the next morning when Gabriel reached the Abbey, to his great joy he found the chain gone (for the Abbot had so ordered after his visit to the chapter-house), and Brother Stephen already hard at

work, and happy as a bird. For like many other artist
souls, when things went wrong, Brother Stephen
suffered dreadful unhappiness; while, on the other
hand, when pleased, he was full of boundless
delight; and so, being relieved from the chain, he
was in one of his most joyous moods.

He smiled brightly as Gabriel entered; and the April
sunlight streaming in through the high narrow
windows sparkled so radiantly, and so filled them
with the life and energy and gladness of the spring-
time, that each of them felt as though he could do
no end of work, and that King Louis's book should
be one of the most beautiful things in all the world!

And that morning was but the beginning of a long
series of happy days that Brother Stephen and
Gabriel were to spend together. At first the monk
knew nothing of how it happened that he was freed
from the humiliation of the chain; but one day he
heard about Gabriel's talk with the Abbot from one
of the brotherhood who had chanced to be in the
garden that morning, and had overheard them.

At first Brother Stephen was rather displeased; for
he did not like it that the little boy had begged of
the Abbot something which he himself was too
proud to ask. But when he thought it over, and
reflected that it was out of sheer kindness that
Gabriel had made the request, his heart strangely
warmed toward the lad. Indeed, through all his life
in the Abbey, no one had ever really cared whether
he was happy or unhappy; and so poor Brother
Stephen had had no idea how very pleasant it would
be to have even a little peasant boy take an interest

in him. And as day after day went by, he began to love Gabriel, as he had never before loved any one.

Yes, those were very happy days for both of them, and very busy ones, too. Every morning Gabriel would come to the Abbey with his hands filled with the prettiest wild flowers he could find on the way; and from these Brother Stephen would select the ones that pleased him best to paint. Sometimes it would be the sweet wild hyacinths of pale blue, sometimes the yellow marsh-marigolds, and again the little deep pink field-roses, or some other of the innumerable lovely blossoms that every season brought. And with them all, as he had said, he put in the small flying creatures; butterflies and bees, scarlet ladybugs and pale green beetles, whose wings looked like scraps of rainbows; and sometimes, in his zeal, he even painted the little snails with their curled-up shells, and the fuzzy caterpillars that happened to come in on Gabriel's bouquets, and you really would never believe how very handsome even these looked in the gold borders, when Brother Stephen got through with them.

And so, day by day, the book grew in perfect beauty. And as Brother Stephen worked, there was much for Gabriel to do also. For in those days artists could not buy their ink and paints all ready for use as they do to-day, but were obliged to prepare by hand almost all their materials; and a little assistant such as Gabriel had to keep his hands busy, and his eyes open, too.

For instance, the matter of the ink alone, Gabriel

had to have on his mind for weeks; for one could not then buy it ready made, in a bottle, as we do now without the least trouble, but the monks or their colour-grinders had to make it themselves.

And this is the way Gabriel had been taught to do it: morning after morning of those early spring days, as he trudged along on his way to the Abbey, he kept sharp watch on the young hawthorn-trees by the roadside; and when their first buds showed, and while they were still tiny, he gathered armfuls of the boughs, and carried them to the Abbey, where he spread them out in a sunny corner of the courtyard to stay until quite dry. Then he had to put them in a stone mortar and pound off all the bark; and this he put to steep in great earthen jars of water, until the water might draw all the sap from out the bark. All this took several weeks to do.

And then Gabriel spent a number of busy days in the great kitchen. There he had a large saucepan, and in it he placed, a little at a time, the water in which the bark was steeping; and then raking out some coals from the blazing fire of logs, he set his saucepan over them, and watched the barky water until it had boiled down very thick, much as one boils down syrup for preserves.

Then he dipped out the thick liquid into little bags of parchment, which he had spent days stitching up very tightly, so that nothing could leak out. After the little bags were filled, he hung them out-of-doors in the bright sunlight; and as the days grew warmer and warmer, the sun soon dried their contents, so that if one of the little bags were opened it would be found filled with a dark powder.

And then, last of all, when Brother Stephen wished some fresh ink for his writing, or for the delicate lines about his initial letters or borders, Gabriel would take a little of the dry powder from one of the bags, and, putting it in a small saucepan over the fire, would melt it with a little wine. And so at last it would be ready for use; a fine, beautiful black ink that hundreds of years have found hard work to fade.

Then there was the gold to grind and prepare; that was the hardest of all, and fairly made his arms ache. Many of the paints, too, had to be worked over very carefully; and the blue especially, and other brilliant colours made from vegetable dyes, must be kept in a very curious way. Brother Stephen would prepare the dyes, as he preferred to do this himself; and then Gabriel would take little pieces of linen cloth and dip a few in each of the colours until the linen would be soaked; and afterward, when they had dried in the sun, he would arrange these bits in a little booklet of cotton paper, which every night Brother Stephen, as was the custom with many of the monks, put under his pillow so that it might keep very dry and warm; for this preserved the colours in all their brightness. And then when he wanted to use some of them, he would tell Gabriel to cut off a bit of the linen of whatever colour he wished, and soak it in water, and in this way he would get a fine liquid paint.

For holding this paint, as dishes were none too plenty in those days, mussel shells were generally used; and one of Gabriel's tasks was to gather numbers of these from the banks of the little river that ran through one of the Abbey meadows. That was very pleasant work, though, and sometimes, late in the afternoons of those lovely summer days, Brother Stephen and Gabriel would walk out together to the edge of this little river; the monk to sit on the grassy bank dreaming of all the beautiful things he meant to paint, while Gabriel hunted for the pretty purple shells.

And oftentimes the lad would bring along a fishing-pole and try his luck at catching an eel; for even this, too, had to do with the making of the book. For Brother Stephen in putting on the gold of his borders, while he generally used white of egg, yet for certain parts preferred a glue made from the skin of an eel; and this Gabriel could make very finely.

So you see there were a great many things for a little colour-grinder to do; yet Gabriel was very industrious, and it often happened that he would finish his tasks for the day, and still have several hours to himself. And this was the best of all; for at such times Brother Stephen, who was getting along finely, would take great pleasure in teaching him to illuminate. He would let the boy take a piece of parchment, and then giving him beautiful letters and bits of borders, would show him how to copy them. Indeed, he took so much pains in his teaching, that very soon Gabriel, who loved the work, and who had a real talent for it, began to be quite skilful, and to make very good designs of his own.

Whenever he did anything especially nice, Brother

Stephen would seem almost as much pleased as if Gabriel were his own boy; and hugging him affectionately, he would exclaim:

"Ah, little one, thou hast indeed the artist soul! And, please God, I will train thy hand so that when thou art a man it shall never know the hard toil of the peasant. Thy pen and brush shall earn a livelihood for thee!" And then he would take more pains than ever to teach Gabriel all the best knowledge of his art.

Nor did Brother Stephen content himself with teaching the boy only to paint; but in his love for him, he desired to do still more. He had no wealth some day to bestow upon him, but he had something that was a very great deal better; for Brother Stephen, like many of the monks of the time, had a good education; and this he determined to share with Gabriel.

He arranged to have him stay at the Abbey for his supper as often as he could be spared from home; and hour after hour of the long summer evenings he spent teaching the lad to read and write, which was really quite a distinction; for it was an accomplishment that none of the peasants, and very few of the lords and ladies of that time possessed. Gabriel was quick and eager to learn, and Brother Stephen gradually added other things to his list of studies, and both of them took the greatest pleasure in the hours thus passed together.

Sometimes they would go out into the garden, and, sitting on one of the quaint stone benches, Brother

Stephen would point out to Gabriel the different stars, or tell him about the fragrant growing plants around them; or, perhaps, repeat to him some dreamy legend of old, old Normandy.

And then, by and by, Gabriel would go home through the perfumed dark, feeling vaguely happy; for all the while, through those pleasant evenings with Brother Stephen, his mind and heart were opening brightly as the yellow primroses, that blossomed by moonlight over all the Abbey meadows.

CHAPTER V.

THE COUNT'S TAX

AND in this happy manner the spring and summer wore away and the autumn came. Brother Stephen felt very cheerful, for the beautiful book grew more beautiful week by week; and he was very proud and happy, because he knew it was the loveliest thing he had ever made.

Indeed, he himself was so cheerful, that as the autumn days, one after another, melted away, it was some little time before he noticed that Gabriel was losing his merriness, and that he had begun to look sad and distressed. And finally, one morning, he came looking so very unhappy, that Brother Stephen asked, with much concern:

"Why, lad, whither have all thy gay spirits taken flight? Art thou ill?"

"Nay, sir," answered Gabriel, sadly; "but oh, Brother Stephen, we are in so much trouble at home!"

At this the monk at once began to question him, and learned that Gabriel's family were indeed in great misfortune.

And this is how it came about: in those days the peasant folk had a very hard time indeed. All of the land through the country was owned by the great nobles; and the poor peasants, who lived on the little farms into which the land was divided, had few rights. They could not even move to another place if they so wished, but were obliged to spend all their lives under the control of whatever nobleman happened to own the estate on which they were born.

They lived in little thatched cottages, and cultivated their bits of land; and as rent for this, each peasant was obliged to help support the great lord who owned everything, and who always lived in a strong castle, with armed men under his command.

The peasants had to raise wheat and vegetables and sheep and cows, so that the people of the castles might eat nice, white bread, and nut cookies and roast meat; though the poor peasants themselves had to be content, day after day, with little more than hard, black bread, and perhaps a single bowl of cabbage or potato soup, from which the whole family would dip with their wooden spoons.

Then, too, the peasants oftentimes had to pay taxes when their noble lord wished to raise money, and even to follow him to war if he so commanded, though this did not often happen.

And now we come to the reason for Gabriel's troubles. It seems that the Count Pierre de Bouchage, to whose estate Gabriel's family belonged, had got into a quarrel with a certain baron who lived near the town of Evreux, and Count Pierre was determined to take his followers and attack the baron's castle; for these private wars were very common in those days.

But Count Pierre needed money to carry on his little war, and so had laid a very heavy tax on the peasants of his estate; and Gabriel's father had been unable to raise the sum of money demanded. For besides Gabriel, there were several little brothers and sisters in the family, Jean and Margot and little Guillaume, who must be clothed and fed; and though the father was honest and hard-working, yet the land of their little farm was poor, and it was all the family could do to find themselves enough on which to live.

When peasant Viaud had begged Count Pierre to release him from the tax, the count, who was hard and unsympathetic, had become angry, and given orders that the greater part of their little farm should be taken from them, and he had seized also their little flock of sheep. This was a grievous loss, for out of the wool that grew on the sheeps' backs,

Gabriel's mother every winter made the warm, homespun clothes for all the family.

Indeed, Count Pierre had no real right to do all this; but in those times, when a noble lord chose to be cruel and unjust, the poor peasants had no way to help matters.

And this was not all of Gabriel's woes; for only a few days after he had told these things to Brother Stephen, when he went home at night, he found his mother crying bitterly, and learned that Count Pierre, who was having some trouble in raising his money, and so had become more merciless than ever, had that day imprisoned his father at the castle, and refused to release him unless some of the tax were paid.

This was the hardest blow of all; and though the other children were too young to understand all that had befallen them, poor Gabriel and his mother were so distressed that neither slept that night; and the next morning when the little boy arose, tired out instead of rested by the long night, he had scarcely the heart to go away to the Abbey, and leave things so miserable at home. But his mother thought it best for him to keep on with his work with Brother Stephen, because of the little sum he earned; and then, too, he felt that he must do his part to help until King Louis's book was finished. After that, he did not know what he could do! He did not know how he could best try to take his father's place and help the family; for, after all, he knew he was only a little boy, and so things seemed very hopeless!

Indeed the grief and poverty that had come upon them at home made Gabriel so sad that Brother Stephen was quite heart-broken, too, for he deeply loved the lad. As he worked, he kept trying all the while to think of some way to help them; but as the monk had passed all his life within the walls of the Abbey, he knew but little of the ways of the outside world; and he had no money of his own, or he would gladly have paid the tax himself.

CHAPTER VI.

GABRIEL'S PRAYER

MEANTIME, though they worked quietly, they were both very industrious; and at last one day, late in October, when the first snow was beginning to fall, Brother Stephen finished the last page of the beautiful book. He gave a sigh as he laid down his paintbrush; not because he was tired, but because in his heart he was really sorry to finish his work, for he knew that then it would soon be taken away, and he hated to part with it.

As he and Gabriel laid all the pages together in the order in which they were to go, brother Stephen's heart swelled with pride, and Gabriel thought he had never seen anything half so lovely!

The text was written in beautiful letters of the lustrous black ink which Gabriel had made; and at the beginnings of new chapters, wonderful initial letters glittered in gold and colours till they looked like little mosaics of precious stones.

Here and there through the text were scattered exquisite miniature pictures of saints and angels; while as for the borders that enclosed every page, they wreathed around the written words such lovely garlands of painted blossoms, that to Gabriel the whole book seemed a marvellous bouquet of all the sweet flowers he had daily gathered from the Norman fields, and that Brother Stephen, by the magic of his art, had made immortal.

Indeed the little boy fairly blinked as he looked at the sparkling beauty of those pages where the blossoms were to live on, through the centuries, bright and beautiful and unharmed by wind or rain or the driving snow, that even then was covering up all the bare frost-smitten meadows without.

And so Gabriel turned over page after page shining with gold and purple and rose-colour, till he came to the very last of the text; and then he saw that there was yet one page more, and on turning over this he read these words:

"I, Brother Stephen, of the Abbey of St. Martin-de-Bouchage, made this book; and for every initial letter and picture and border of flowers that I have herein wrought, I pray the Lord God to have compassion upon some one of my grievous sins!"

This was written in beautifully, and all around it was painted a graceful border like braided ribbons of blue.

Now in Brother Stephen's time, when any one
finished an especially beautiful illumination of any
part of the Bible, it was quite customary for the
artist to add, at the end, a little prayer. Indeed, no
one can make a really beautiful thing without loving
the work; and those old-time artist-monks took such
delight in the flowery pages they painted, that they
felt sure the dear Lord himself could not help but be
pleased to have his words made so beautiful, and
that he would so grant the little prayer at the end of
the book, because of the loving labour that had gone
before.

As Gabriel again read over Brother Stephen's last
page, it set him to thinking; and a little later, as he
walked home in the frosty dusk, he thought of it
again.

It was true, he said to himself, that all the beautiful
written and painted work on King Louis's book had
been done by Brother Stephen's hands,--and yet,--
and yet,--had not he, too, helped? Had he not
gathered the thorny hawthorn, and pricked his
fingers, and spent days and days making the ink?
Had he not, week after week, ground the colours
and the gold till his arms ached, and his hands were
blistered? Had he not made the glue, and prepared
the parchment, and ruled the lines (and one had to
be *so* careful not to blot them!), and brought all the
flowers for the borders?

Surely, he thought, though he had not painted any
of its lovely pages, yet he had done his little part to
help make the book, and so, perhaps--perhaps--
might not the Lord God feel kindly toward him, too,

and be willing to grant a little prayer to him also?

Now of course Gabriel could have prayed any time and anywhere, and simply asked for what he wanted. But he had a strong feeling that God would be much more apt to notice it, if the prayer were beautifully written out, like Brother Stephen's, and placed in the book itself, on the making of which he had worked so long and so hard.

Gabriel was very pleased with his idea, and by the time he reached home, he had planned out just what he wanted to say. He ate his supper of hard black bread very happily, and when, soon after, he crept into bed and pulled up his cover of ragged sheepskin, he went to sleep with his head so full of the work of the past few months, that he dreamed that the whole world was full of painted books and angels with rose-coloured wings; that all the meadows of Normandy were covered with gold, and the flowers fastened on with white of egg and eel-skins; and then, just as he was getting out his ruler to rule lines over the blue sky, he rubbed his eyes and woke up; and, finding it was morning, he jumped out of bed, and hastened to make himself ready for his day's work.

When he reached the Abbey, Brother Stephen was busy binding together the finished leaves of the book; for the monks had to do not only the painting, but also the putting together of their books themselves.

After Gabriel had waited on Brother Stephen for awhile, the latter told him he could have some time

to himself, and so he hurried to get out the little jars
of scarlet and blue and black ink, and the bits of
parchment that Brother Stephen had given him. He
looked over the parchment carefully, and at last
found one piece from which he could cut a page
that was almost as large as the pages of the book. It
was an old piece, and had some writing on one side,
but he knew how to scrape it off clean; and then
taking some of the scarlet ink, he ruled some lines
in the centre of the page, and between these, in the
nicest black letters he knew how to make, he wrote
his little prayer. And this is the way it read:

"I, Gabriel Viaud, am Brother Stephen's colour-
grinder; and I have made the ink for this book, and
the glue, and caught the eels, and ground the gold
and colours, and ruled the lines and gathered the
flowers for the borders, and so I pray the Lord God
will be kind and let my father out of prison in Count
Pierre's castle, and tell Count Pierre to give us back
our meadow and sheep, for we cannot pay the tax,
and mother says we will starve."

Now in the little prayers that the monks added at the
end of a book, it was the custom to ask only that
their sins might be forgiven. But Gabriel, though he
knew he had plenty of sins,--for so the parish priest
of St. Martin's village told all the peasant folk every
Sunday,--yet somehow could not feel nearly so
anxious to have them forgiven, as he was to have
his father freed from prison in the castle, and their
little farm and flock restored to them; and so he had
decided to word his prayer the way he did.

It took him some time to write it out, for he took

great pains to shape every letter as perfectly as possible. Nor did he forget that Brother Stephen had taught him always to make the word God more beautiful than the others; so he wrote that in scarlet ink, and edged it with scallops and loops and little dots of blue; and then all around the whole prayer he made graceful flourishes of the coloured inks. He very much wished for a bit of gold with which to enrich his work, but gold was too precious for little boys to practise with, and so Brother Stephen had not given him any for his own. Nevertheless, when the page was finished, the artistic effect was very pleasing, and it really was a remarkably clever piece of work for a little boy to have made.

He did not tell Brother Stephen what he was doing, for he was afraid that perhaps he might not quite approve of his plan. Not that Gabriel wished for a moment to do anything that Brother Stephen would not like him to do, but only that he thought their affairs at home so desperate that he could not afford to risk losing this means of help;--and then, too, he felt that the prayer was his own little secret, and he did not want to tell any one about it anyway.

And so he was greatly relieved that Brother Stephen, who was very much absorbed in his own work, did not ask him any questions. The monk was always very kind about helping him in every way possible, but never insisted on Gabriel's showing him everything, wisely thinking that many times it was best to let the boy work out his own ideas. So Gabriel said nothing about his page, but put it carefully away, until he could find some opportunity to place it in the book itself.

Meantime Brother Stephen worked industriously, and in a few days more he had quite finished the book. He had strongly bound all his painted pages together, and put on a cover of violet velvet, which the nuns of a near-by convent had exquisitely embroidered in pearls and gold. And, last of all, the cover was fastened with clasps of wrought gold, set with amethysts. Altogether it was a royal gift, and one worthy of any queen. Even the Abbot, cold and stately though he usually was, exclaimed with pleasure when he saw it, and warmly praised Brother Stephen upon the loveliness of his work.

CHAPTER VII.

THE BOOK GOES TO LADY ANNE

AND it was well that the beautiful book was finished, for the very next afternoon a nobleman, with several attendants, arrived at the Abbey to see if the work were done. The nobleman was Count Henri of Lisieux, who had been sent by King Louis to bear to Lady Anne a precious casket of jewels as part of his bridal gifts to her; and the count had also received orders from the king to go to St. Martin's Abbey on his way, and if the book of hours were finished, to take it along to the Lady Anne.

Count Henri was greatly pleased when they showed the work to him, and he said that he knew both King Louis and his bride could not help but be delighted with it. And then, after it had been duly looked at and admired, the book was wrapped up in a piece of soft, rich silk and laid on a shelf in the chapter-house to wait until the next morning, when Count Henri would take it away. For he had come far, and the Abbot had invited him to stay overnight in the Abbey before going on with his journey.

While all this was taking place, and the book was being examined, Gabriel had been quietly at work in one corner of the chapter-house, grinding some gold; and when he heard that Count Henri was going away the next morning, he knew that if he expected to put his own little page in the book, he must do so some time before he went home that evening; and he did not quite see how he could manage it.

Late in the afternoon, however, a little before dusk, all the others left the chapter-house, Brother Stephen to go to his own cell, while the Abbot took Count Henri out to show him over the Abbey. And just as soon as they were gone, Gabriel hastily put down the stone mortar in which he was grinding the gold, and, going over to the work-table, opened the drawer in which he kept his own things, and took out the page on which he had written his little prayer.

He then went to the shelf and took down the book. He felt guilty as he unfolded the silk wrappings, and his hands trembled as he loosened the golden clasps, and hurriedly slipped in his piece of parchment. He put it in at the very back of the book, after Brother Stephen's last page. Then carefully refastening the clasps, and again folding it up in its silken cover, he replaced the book on the shelf.

Poor Gabriel did not know whether he had done very wrong or not in taking this liberty with the painted book. He only knew that he could not bear to have it go away without his little prayer between its covers; and he thought that now God would surely notice it, as he had written it as nicely as he knew how, and had placed it next to Brother Stephen's.

By this time it was growing dark, and so Gabriel left the Abbey and took his way home. When he reached their forlorn little cottage, he found only a scanty supper awaiting him, and very early he went to bed; for they had but little fire and were too poor to afford even a single candle to burn through the long winter evening.

As Gabriel lay shivering in his cold little bed, he wondered how long it would be before God would grant his prayer for help. And then he wondered if God would be displeased because he had dared to put it in the beautiful book without asking permission from Brother Stephen or the Abbot. And the more he thought of the possibility of this, and of all their other troubles, the more miserable he felt, till at last he sobbed himself to sleep.

The poor little boy did not know that after he himself had been sleeping for several hours, Brother Stephen, who had not slept, came out of his cell in the Abbey, and, carrying in his hand a small lamp, passed softly down the corridor and into the chapter-house. For Brother Stephen, like many another true artist who has worked long and lovingly upon some exquisite thing, found it very hard to part with that which he had made. He did not expect ever again to see the beautiful book after it left the Abbey, and so he felt that he must take a farewell look at it all by himself.

As he entered the chapter-house, he set the lamp on the table; and then taking down the book and placing it also on the table, he unwrapped and unclasped it, and seating himself in front of it, looked long and earnestly at each page as he slowly turned them over, one by one.

When at last he came to the end, and found a loose leaf, he picked it up in dismay, wondering if his binding could have been so badly done that one of the pages had already become unfastened. But his look of dismay changed to bewilderment as he examined the page more closely, and saw Gabriel's little prayer. He read this over twice, very slowly; and then, still holding the page in his hand, he sat for a long time with his head bowed; and once or twice something that looked very like a tear fell on the stone floor at his feet.

After awhile the lamp began to burn low; and Brother Stephen rising, gave a tender look to the loose page he had been holding, and then carefully put it back in the book, taking pains to place it, as nearly as he could, exactly as Gabriel had done. Then, with a sigh, he shut the velvet covers, once more fastened the golden clasps, and, replacing the silken wrappings, laid the book on the shelf, and went back to his cell.

The next morning Count Henri and his escort made
ready for their journey to Bretagne. Count Henri
himself placed the precious book in the same velvet
bag which held the casket of jewels for the Lady
Anne, and this bag he hung over his saddle-bow
directly in front of him, so that he could keep close
watch and see that no harm befell King Louis's
gifts.

And then he and his soldiers mounted their horses,
and, taking a courteous leave of the Abbot and the
brotherhood of St. Martin's, they trotted off along
the frosty road.

CHAPTER VIII.

LADY ANNE WRITES TO THE KING

AFTER several days' journey they entered
Bretagne, and before long drew near to the city of
Nantes and the castle of Lady Anne. This castle was
very large, and had many towers and gables and
little turrets with sharp-pointed, conical roofs.
There was a high wall and a moat all around it, and
as Count Henri approached, he displayed a little
banner given him by King Louis, and made of blue
silk embroidered with three golden lilies.

At the sight of this, the keepers of the drawbridge
(who in those days always had to be very watchful
not to admit enemies to their lord's castle) instantly
lowered the bridge, and Count Henri and his guard

rode over and were respectfully received within the gate.

They dismounted in the courtyard, and then, after resting awhile in one of the rooms of the castle, Count Henri was escorted into the great hall of state, where Lady Anne was ready to receive him.

This hall was very large and handsome, with a high, arched ceiling, and walls hung with wonderful old tapestries. Standing about in groups were numbers of picturesquely dressed pages, ladies-in-waiting, richly clad, and Breton gentlemen gorgeous in velvets and lace ruffles, for a hundred of these always attended Lady Anne wherever she went. At one end of the hall was a dais spread with cloth of gold, and there, in a carved chair, sat the Lady Anne herself. She wore a beautiful robe of brocaded crimson velvet, and over her dark hair was a curious, pointed head-dress of white silk embroidered with pearls and gold thread.

As Count Henri approached, she greeted him very cordially; and then, kneeling before her, he said:

"My Lady, I have the happiness to deliver to your hands these bridal gifts which our gracious sovereign, King Louis, did me the honour to entrust to my care."

And then, as he handed to her the casket of jewels and the silken package containing the hour book, she replied:

"Sir Count, I thank you for your courtesy in bearing

these gifts to me, and I am well pleased to receive them."

Then summoning a little page, she told him to carry the presents up to her own chamber, where she might examine them at her leisure.

By and by, Count Henri withdrew, after asking permission to start the next morning on his return to Paris; for he wished to report to the king that he had safely accomplished his errand.

And then Lady Anne, having given orders that he and his followers be hospitably entertained during their stay in the castle, mounted the great stone staircase, and went to her own room, for she very much wanted to look at the gifts from King Louis.

These she found on a table where the little page had placed them. The casket was uncovered, while the book was still wrapped up in the piece of silk, so that one could not tell just what it was.

Lady Anne opened the casket first, as it happened to be nearest to her; and she drew in her breath, and her eyes sparkled with pleasure, as she lifted out a magnificent necklace, and other rich jewels that gleamed and glittered in the light like blue and crimson fires. She tried on all the ornaments, and then, after awhile, when she had admired them to her heart's content, she took up the silk-covered package, and curiously unwrapped it. When she saw what it contained, however, her face grew radiant with delight, and--

"Ah!" she exclaimed to herself, "King Louis's gifts are indeed princely, and this one is the most royal of all!"

For King Louis had been entirely right in thinking nothing would please the Lady Anne quite so much as a piece of fine illumination.

Still holding the book carefully in her hands, she at once seated herself in a deep, cushioned chair, and began slowly to turn over the pages, taking the keenest pleasure, as she did so, in every fresh beauty on which her eyes fell. When she had gone about half through the book, she lifted it up to look more closely at an especially beautiful initial letter, and then, all at once, out fluttered the loose leaf which Gabriel had put in.

As it fell to the floor, a little page near by hastened to pick it up, and, bending on one knee, presented it to Lady Anne. At first she frowned a little, for she thought, as had Brother Stephen, that the book must have been badly bound. But when she took the leaf in her hand, to her surprise, she saw that it was different from the others, and that it had not been bound in with them; and then she read over the writing very carefully. When she had finished, she sat for some time, just as Brother Stephen had done, holding the page in her hand, while her face wore a very tender expression.

Lady Anne was really deeply touched by Gabriel's little prayer, and she wished greatly that she herself might find a way to help him and his family out of their trouble.

But the more she thought about it, she realized that she had no authority over a Norman nobleman, and that no one in France, except the king, was powerful enough to compel Count Pierre to release the peasant Viaud from imprisonment.

So going over to a little writing-table, she took out a thin sheet of parchment, a quaint goose-quill pen, and a small horn full of ink, and wrote a letter which she addressed to King Louis. Then she took the loose leaf on which Gabriel's prayer was written, and, folding it in with her letter, tied the little packet with a thread of scarlet silk (for no one used envelopes then), and sealed it with some red wax. And on the wax she pressed a carved ring which she wore, and which left a print that looked like a tiny tuft of ermine fur encircled by a bit of knotted cord; for this was Lady Anne's emblem, as it was called, and King Louis, seeing it, would know at once that the packet came from her.

Then she went down into the great hall of the castle, and sent one of her Breton gentlemen to bring Count Henri. When the latter entered, she said to him:

"Sir Count, it would give me great pleasure to keep you longer as my guest, but if you must return to Paris tomorrow, I will ask you to be my bearer for a little packet which I am anxious to send to King Louis."

Then, as she handed it to him, she added with a smile, "I give it to you now, for if you ride early in the morning, I must leave my Breton gentlemen to do the honours of your stirrup-cup."

(This last was the cup of wine which it was considered polite to offer a departing guest as he mounted his horse, and was a little ceremony over which Lady Anne liked to preside herself; that is, when her guests went away at agreeable hours.)

As Count Henri received the packet from her, he made a very deep bow, and replied that he would be most happy to serve the Lady Anne in any way he could, and that he only awaited her command to start at once on his journey.

"Nay," said Lady Anne, with another little smile, "'tis no affair of state importance! Only a matter of my own on which I have set my heart. But I will not hear to your setting forth, until you have sat at my table and rested overnight in the castle."

To this Count Henri again gallantly bowed his obedience; and then, before long, Lady Anne led all the company into the great banquet-hall, where a number of long tables were set out with roasted game, and bread and wine and the many different cakes and sweetmeats of Bretagne.

The Lady Anne took her place at the head of the longest table of all, and she placed Count Henri at her right hand. Near them sat many of the ladies-in-waiting, and Breton gentlemen of the highest rank; while at the farther end, beyond a great silver saltcellar standing in the middle of the table, were seated those of less degree.

The dishes were of gold and silver, and Lady Anne
herself was waited upon by two noblemen of
Bretagne, for she lived very magnificently, as was
fitting for the bride of King Louis.

When the supper was over, they all went back into
the great castle hall, where bright fires of logs were
blazing in the huge fireplaces; and as they sat in the
firelight, they listened to the beautiful songs and
music of two troubadours who had that day chanced
to come to the castle, and who sang so sweetly that
it was very late before the company broke up for the
night.

All through the evening, however, in spite of the
pleasant entertainment, Lady Anne, who was very
sympathetic, could not help but think many times of
poor little Gabriel, and how cold and hungry and
miserable he must be! She had been much struck,
too, with the beautiful way in which he had written
out and ornamented his little prayer, for she was a
good judge of such things; and, as she thought
about it, she determined some day to see the lad
herself. Meantime she was very anxious to help him
as soon as possible. Indeed, she felt much happier
when the next morning came, and Count Henri set
out for Paris; for then she knew that her letter and
Gabriel's little written page were on their way to
King Louis.

In due time, Count Henri arrived safely at the king's
palace, and delivered the packet from Lady Anne.
And when King Louis broke the wax seal, and read
the letter and Gabriel's little prayer, he, too, was
deeply touched. Lady Anne's letter explained to him

about finding the loose page in the beautiful book
he had sent her, and asked that he would see to it
that Count Pierre set the boy's father free.

This King Louis at once determined to do, for he
was a just and kind-hearted monarch, and during his
reign did much to lighten the taxes and oppression
of the peasant-folk; and, moreover, in this trouble of
Gabriel's father, he now took an especial interest, as
it gave him great pleasure to grant any wish of the
Lady Anne, whom he loved deeply.

So that very day he sent for a trusty messenger, and
after explaining things to him, directed him to set
out as soon as possible for St. Martin's Abbey, and
there to seek out Brother Stephen and inquire about
the little peasant boy, Gabriel Viaud. And then, if
he found everything to be true that Gabriel had said
in his prayer, he was to act according to further
orders which King Louis gave him.

CHAPTER IX.

THE KING'S MESSENGER

NOW while all these things had been going on,
poor Gabriel had been growing more wretchedly
unhappy day by day. His people had become poorer
and poorer, and the long, cold winter was upon
them. They had almost given up hope of the release
of peasant Viaud from prison, and did not know
where they could get bread or fire to keep them

alive through the bitter cold. Sometimes Gabriel thought with despair of how much he had hoped from his little prayer! For he was sure, by this time, that God was angry with him for daring to put it in the beautiful book.

And to add the last touch to his distress, he had been obliged to give up his work and lessons at the Abbey; for Brother Stephen had been ill for a time, and unable to paint, and all the other monks had colour-grinders of their own. So Gabriel, who could not afford to be idle even for a few days, had been forced to seek employment elsewhere.

The only work he could find was with a leather dresser in the village of St. Martin's, and though it was very hard and distasteful to him, he felt that he must keep at it, as he could thus earn a few pennies more each day than he could as colour-grinder at the Abbey. And yet, with all his hard toil, the little sum he brought home at night was far from enough to keep them all from want, to say nothing of paying the tax which still hung over them; and so every day they became more hopeless and discouraged.

Indeed, in those times, when a peasant family fell under the displeasure of their noble lord, it was a bitter misfortune, for there were few places to which they might turn for help.

And it seemed to Gabriel especially hard to bear all their troubles in the gracious Christmas season; for it was now past the middle of December. Always before they had had enough for their happy little Christmas feast, and some to spare. They had always had their sheaf of wheat put by for the birds; and for two seasons past Gabriel's father had let him climb up the tall ladder and fasten the holiday sheaf, bound with its garland of greens, to the roof of the little peaked and gabled dovecote that stood on top of a carved pole in the centre of the farmyard. For every Norman peasant always wishes the birds, too, to be happy at the joyous Christmas-tide.

And always, every Christmas eve, when Gabriel and his little brothers and sister had gone to bed, they had set their wooden shoes in a row on the hearthstone; and then in the morning when they wakened up, they always found that the blessed Christ-child had been there in the night, and filled all the little shoes with red apples and nuts.

But this Christmas-time everything was so sad and changed, they were sure even the Christ-child would forget them. And, day by day, the little supply of coarse meal for their black bread grew smaller and smaller, and the snow became deeper, and the wintry winds blew more cold and cruelly.

Meantime, King Louis's messenger was travelling as fast as he could, and three days before Christmas he arrived at St. Martin's Abbey. The Abbot was greatly surprised to see him, and still more so when he asked if he might speak privately with Brother Stephen. This the Abbot granted, though he was very anxious to know the messenger's errand; for he could think of no reason for it, unless there had been something wrong with King Louis's book. So he was quite uneasy as he saw the messenger enter Brother Stephen's cell and close the door.

Brother Stephen, too, was at first much surprised
when his visitor told him he had come from King
Louis to inquire about a peasant boy by the name of
Gabriel Viaud; though in a moment it flashed
through his mind that Gabriel's prayer had found its
way to the palace, and that the answer was coming.

He said nothing of this, however, but when the
messenger asked if he had had such a boy for
colour-grinder, he eagerly answered:

"Yes, and there lives no manlier and sweeter-
spirited lad in all France!"

"Is it true," continued the messenger, "that Count
Pierre de Bouchage hath imprisoned his father for
failure to pay a tax, and that the family are now in
sore distress?"

"Yes, that also is true," replied the monk very sadly.
And then he said beseechingly: "But surely King
Louis will help them? Surely our gracious sovereign
will not allow such injustice and cruelty?"

Here the messenger answered:

"Nay, our sovereign is indeed a generous monarch!
Else had he not been touched by the little prayer
which the peasant lad placed in the book thou
madest for the Lady Anne. Though I dare say thou
knewest naught of it" (here Brother Stephen smiled
gently, but said nothing), "yet so the lad did. And
'twas because of that scrap of parchment falling
under the eyes of King Louis, that I have journeyed
all the way from Paris. And," he added, as he

remembered the heavy snow through which he had ridden, "it takes a stout heart and a stouter horse to brave thy Norman roads in December!"

Then he asked Brother Stephen a great many more questions, and inquired what road to take in order to find Count Pierre's castle, and also the Viaud cottage. And then when he had satisfied himself about all these matters, he went back to the great hall of the Abbey, where the Abbot was slowly pacing the floor, telling his beads as he walked.

The Abbot, though very curious as to the reason of the messenger's visit, asked him no questions other than if the book for Lady Anne had been entirely satisfactory; and he felt relieved when the messenger assured him that so far as he knew both the king and Lady Anne had been greatly delighted with it. Then, after talking a little while about Brother Stephen's artistic work, the messenger briefly explained to the Abbot his errand, and told him that King Louis had ordered him to make his inquiries about Gabriel as quietly as possible.

As he heard, the Abbot raised his eyebrows and looked somewhat disapproving, when he realized that the peasant lad who had dared to put his page into the beautiful book was the same little colour-grinder who had had the boldness to speak to him, one day in the garden, and ask him to take off Brother Stephen's chain. However, whatever he may have thought, he kept it to himself; he treated the messenger with much courtesy, and, on bidding him good night, invited him to stay as a guest of the Abbey so long as he chose.

The next morning the messenger rode to the Viaud farm, and, though he did not go into the cottage, he looked it over carefully and the land about it; and then he took the highway that led to the castle of Count Pierre de Bouchage.

When he reached the castle, he asked to see Count Pierre, and so was taken into the great hall, where the count received him in a very haughty manner. He became somewhat more polite, however, when he learned that King Louis had sent the messenger to him; though he looked decidedly blank when the latter presented to him a letter written on parchment and fastened with a wax seal stamped with the king's emblem, which was the print of a little porcupine with the quills on his back standing up straight, and a crown on top of them.

On seeing this letter, Count Pierre looked blank because the truth was, that, like many other noble lords at that time, he could read only with great difficulty. But then the messenger rather expected this, and so he asked permission to read the parchment to him, and Count Pierre frowningly assented.

Indeed, though the messenger pretended not to notice his angry looks, he frowned blacker and blacker as the reading went on. For King Louis requested in the letter that Count Pierre at once release from prison in his castle one Jacques Viaud, peasant on his estate. And the king further said that he himself wished to buy the Viaud cottage and farm, together with a good-sized piece of ground that adjoined it (the messenger, in looking it over that morning, had selected a piece of land which was much better soil than the most of the Viaud farm), and he stated that for this purpose he had sent by his messenger a certain sum in gold pieces.

The king mentioned also that he would like to have the flock of sheep, with the addition of fifty more than had been taken from them, restored to the Viaud family. And, finally, he said that he desired Count Pierre to do these things in honour of his king's approaching marriage with the Lady Anne. For when kings and queens marry, it is generally customary for them, and for many of the loyal noblemen who are their subjects, to bestow gifts and benefits upon the poor people, so that every one may be as happy as possible on the royal wedding-day.

Now Count Pierre really did not care a fig to do honour to King Louis's marriage, and he was very angry to be asked to release a peasant whom he had imprisoned, and to restore flocks which he had seized; and especially was he furious at the request to buy the land, for he did not wish to sell it, and so to lose control over the peasant-folk who lived there.

But, nevertheless, in spite of his wrath, the count knew well enough that he had no real right to do as he had done, and that King Louis knew it also; and that therefore the very best thing he could do was to obey the king's wishes at once.

King Louis had made his letter a polite request rather than a command, because some of his unruly subjects, like Count Pierre, were proud and difficult to manage, and he wished to settle matters pleasantly and peaceably, if possible. And so, in asking him to honour the royal wedding, he gave the count an excuse to yield to his king's wishes, without hurting his pride so much as if he were obliged to obey a command.

Count Pierre began to see this, too; and, moreover, he knew that, notwithstanding the politeness of his letter, the king had plenty of soldiers, and that he would not hesitate to send them to the Castle de Bouchage, if necessary, to bring its lord to terms. And he very wisely reflected that to fight King Louis would be a much more dangerous and expensive undertaking than the private war with the Baron of Evreux, which he already had on his hands.

Before yielding to the requests in the letter, however, Count Pierre wished to satisfy himself that the messenger had correctly read it to him. And so, haughtily demanding it for a few minutes, he hurried out of the hall, and sent a page scampering off to bring to him a troubadour; for one or more of these wandering singers were always to be found in every nobleman's castle, and the count knew that most of them could read.

When in a few minutes the page came back, followed, close at his heels, by a man in motley dress, with a viol hung over his shoulders, Count Pierre, without waiting to greet the latter, thrust the parchment into his hands with the gruff command:

"There, fellow! read this letter for me instantly! and if thou makest a single mistake, I will have thee strangled with the strings of thine own viol, and tumbled off the highest turret of this castle before set of sun!"

At this fierce threat, the troubadour began at once to read, taking care to make no mistakes. Count Pierre listened attentively to every word, and when the troubadour came to the end, having read it exactly as the messenger had done, the count angrily snatched it from his hands, and, swallowing his rage as best he could, went slowly back to the castle hall.

Then, after a few moments' silence, he very ungraciously and ill-naturedly gave orders that peasant Viaud be released from prison, and the sheep sent back. He made a very wry face over the fifty extra ones, and did not look at all anxious to celebrate King Louis's approaching wedding.

And then he took the gold pieces which the messenger offered him, and reluctantly scrawled his name (it was all he could write, and that very badly) to a piece of parchment which the messenger had ready, and which, when Count Pierre had signed it, proved that he had sold to King Louis the land and cottage, and no longer held control over peasant Viaud or any of his family.

When this was done, the messenger, bidding the nobleman a courteous farewell, left the latter still very angry and scowling, and, above all, lost in amazement that King Louis should take all this trouble on account of a poor, unknown peasant, who had lived all his life on a tiny farm in Normandy! And as no one ever explained things to him, Count Pierre never did know how it had all come about, and that, however much against his will, he was doing his part toward helping answer Gabriel's little prayer.

CHAPTER X.

GABRIEL'S CHRISTMAS

WHEN the messenger reached the courtyard of the castle, he found peasant Viaud awaiting him there. The poor man looked very pale and wan from his imprisonment, and his face pitifully showed what anxiety he had suffered in thinking about his family left with no one to help them. His clothes, too, were thin and worn, and he shivered in the cold December wind. Noticing this, the messenger at once sent word to Count Pierre that he was sure King Louis would be highly gratified, if, in further honour of his coming marriage, the count would supply peasant Viaud with a warm suit of clothes before leaving the castle.

This message was almost too much for Count Pierre to bear, but he did not dare to refuse. And the messenger smiled to himself when, by and by, a page came and called Gabriel's father into the castle, from which, in a little while, he came out, warmly clad, and quite bewildered at all that was happening to him.

As they set out together for the Viaud cottage, peasant Viaud walking, and the messenger riding very slowly, the latter explained to him all about Gabriel's little prayer in the beautiful book, and how Lady Anne had sent it to King Louis, to whom he owed his release from prison. But the messenger added that, aside from the lad's father and mother, the king did not wish any one, not even Gabriel himself, to know how it had all come about.

For King Louis declared that he himself did not deserve any thanks, but that the good God had only chosen the Lady Anne and himself and Count Pierre (though the latter did not know it) as the means of answering Gabriel's prayer, and of helping the Christ-child bring happiness at the blessed Christmas-time. For King Louis had not forgotten that the great day was near at hand.

Of the promised return of the sheep, and the buying of the farm by the king, the messenger said nothing then; and when they had nearly reached the cottage, he took leave of peasant Viaud and rode back to the Abbey. For, having finished the king's errand, before going away, he wanted to say good-bye to the Abbot and brothers of St. Martin's, and also to get some of his belongings which he had left at the Abbey.

A few minutes after the messenger had left him, peasant Viaud reached the cottage and raised the latch,--but then it is no use trying to tell how surprised and happy they all were! how they hugged and kissed each other, and laughed and cried!

And then, when the first excitement was over, they began soberly to wonder what they would do next; for they still feared the displeasure of Count Pierre, and still did not know where to turn to raise the tax, or to help their poverty.

"If only he had not taken the sheep," said Gabriel's mother, sadly, "at least I could have spun warm clothes for all of us!"

But even as she spoke, a loud "Baa! Baa!" sounded from up the road, and presently along came a large flock of sheep followed by one of Count Pierre's shepherds, who, without saying a word to any one, skilfully guided them into the Viaud sheepfold, and there safely penned them in; then, still without a word, he turned about and went off in the direction of the castle.

Gabriel's father and mother, who from the cottage window had watched all this in silent amazement, looked at each other, too bewildered to speak. Then they went out together to the sheepfold, and peasant Viaud, who began to realize that this, too, must be part of King Louis's orders, explained to his wife that which the messenger had told him. When he had finished, they went back, hand in hand, to the house, their eyes filled with happy tears, and in their hearts a great tenderness for the little son who had brought help to them.

Just before dark, that same afternoon, the king's messenger, having taken leave of the Abbey folk, once more passed along the highroad. On his way, he was particular to stop at the Viaud cottage,

where he contrived to have a few minutes' talk
alone with Gabriel's mother, and then wishing her a
merry Christmas, he spurred his horse, and rode
along on his journey back to Paris.

As he neared St. Martin's village, he passed a little
peasant boy, in a worn blouse, walking toward the
country; and had he known that this same lad was
the Gabriel because of whom, at King Louis's order,
he had ridden all the way from Paris, he would
certainly have looked at the boy with keen interest.

While for his part, had Gabriel known that the
strange horseman was a messenger from the king,
and that he had that day played a very important
part in the affairs of the Viaud family,--had he
known this,--he surely would have stood stock-still
and opened his eyes wide with amazement!

But the messenger was absorbed in his own
thoughts, and so rode swiftly on; while poor Gabriel
was too sad and wretched to pay much attention to
any one.

As the lad drew near home, however, all at once he
fancied he heard the bleating of sheep. At this he
pricked up his ears and began to run, his heart
suddenly beating very fast with excitement!

When he reached the sheepfold, sure enough, there
was no mistaking the sounds within. He opened the
door and hurried through the thatched shed, noting
with delight the rows of woolly backs glistening in
the twilight, and then, bursting into the cottage,
rushed up to his father and kissed and hugged him

with all his might!

Indeed, Gabriel was so happy and excited that he
did not realize that he was not at all surprised with
their good fortune. For miserable as he had been for
weeks, and though he had thought that he had quite
despaired of his prayer being answered, yet deep
down in his heart, without knowing it, all the while
he had cherished a strong hope that it would be.

Nor was Brother Stephen surprised either, when, at
barely daybreak the next morning, before going to
his work, Gabriel hurried up to the Abbey and told
him all about it. His face beamed with delight,
however, and he seemed almost as happy over it all
as Gabriel himself. He smiled, too, but said nothing,
as the lad wondered over and over what God had
done to Count Pierre, to make him willing to free
his father and restore the sheep! He only said, as he
gently patted Gabriel's hair:

"There, there, little one! the good God hath many
ways of softening men's hearts, and never thou
mind in what manner he hath chosen to manage the
Count Pierre!"

Just then one of the monks went past the open door,
his arms full of evergreens, and carrying in his hand
a pot of the pretty white flowers that the Norman
peasant folk call Christmas roses. Seeing him,
Brother Stephen told Gabriel that he must go and
help the brothers trim the Abbey church for the
joyous service of the morrow; and so with another
affectionate little pat, he went out to do his part in
arranging the holiday greens and garlands and tall

wax candles, while Gabriel hurried off to his work
in the village.

The little boy was so happy, though, over the things
that had happened at home, that he went about all
day in a sort of wondering dream. And that evening
as he went home from his work, very tired, but still
dreaming, the early Christmas-eve stars shone and
twinkled so radiantly over his head and the snow
sparkled so brightly under his feet, that he fairly
tingled through and through with the nameless,
magic happiness of the blessed season!

And when he reached home, and sat down next to
his father while they ate their scanty supper, they all
felt so glad to be together again that nobody minded
that the pieces of black bread were smaller than
ever, and that when the cold wind blew through the
crevices of the cottage walls, there was not enough
fire on the hearth to keep them from shivering.

Indeed, they were all so much happier than they had
been for many weeks, that when Gabriel and the
younger children went to bed, the latter, with many
little gurgles of laughter, arranged their little
wooden shoes on the hearth, just as they had always
done on Christmas eve.

For they said to each other, Jean, and Margot, and
little Guillaume, that surely the good God had not
forgotten them after all! Had he not brought back
their father and the sheep? And surely he would tell
the little Christ-child to bring them a few Christmas
apples and nuts!

Gabriel, however, took no part in their talk, and he did not set his shoes on the hearth with the others; not that he feared they would be forgotten, but rather because he thought that he had already asked for so much and been so generously answered, that he had had his share of Christmas happiness.

His father was freed from prison, and the flock of sheep, with fifty more than they had had before, were back in the fold; and though they were not yet relieved from the tax, nor was their land restored to them, as he had prayed, yet he felt sure that these, too, would come about in some way.

And so, considering all these things, he did not quite like to set out his wooden shoes, and thus invite the Christ-child to give him more; for he knew the Christ-child had a great many shoes to attend to that night. So Gabriel, as he made himself ready for bed, pretended not to hear the chatter of his little brothers and sister, nor to notice what they were doing.

When peasant Viaud, however, saw them standing their little empty shoes in front of the meagre fire, he bowed his head on his hands, and the tears trickled through his fingers. But the mother smiled softly to herself, as she kissed each of the children and tucked them into their worn sheepskin covers.

Next morning, at the first peep of day, every one in the cottage was wide awake; and as soon as they opened their eyes, the children all jumped out of bed and ran to the hearth with little screams of delight. For there stood the little wooden shoes,--

Gabriel's, too, though he had not put them there,--
and even a larger one apiece for the father and
mother, and the blessed Christ-child had not
forgotten one!

Only instead of apples and nuts, they were filled
with the most wonderful bonbons; strange sugar
birds, and animals, and candied fruits such as no
peasant child in Normandy had ever before seen; for
they were sweetmeats that no one but the cooks of
old Paris knew just how to make.

And then, as with eager fingers the children drew
out these marvels, down in the toe of each shoe they
found a little porcupine of white sugar with pink
quills tipped with a tiny, gilded, candy crown; and
last of all, after each little porcupine, out tumbled a
shining yellow gold piece stamped with the likeness
of King Louis.

Even the larger shoes were filled with bonbons, too,
and from the toe of the mother's out dropped a gold
piece, like the others, only larger. But when the
father, with clumsy hands, emptied his shoe, instead
of a gold piece, there fell out a small parchment roll
fastened with a silken cord, and showing at one
corner a wax seal bearing the print of the little royal
porcupine and crown.

Peasant Viaud gazed at it for a few minutes, in utter
bewilderment, and then handing it to Gabriel, who
was standing by, he said:

"Here, child, 'tis a bit of writing, and thou art the
only one of us who can read. See if Brother

Stephen's lessons have taken thee far enough to
make out the meaning of this!"

Gabriel took the roll and eagerly untied the cord,
and then he carefully spelled out every word of the
writing, which was signed by Count Pierre de
Bouchage.

For it was the very same parchment which King
Louis's messenger had made Count Pierre sign to
prove that he had sold to the king, for a certain sum
of gold, the old Viaud farm, together with a piece of
good land adjoining it; and then, at the end of the
deed, as the writing was called, there were a few
lines from King Louis himself, which said that in
honour of the blessed Christmas-time the king took
pleasure in presenting to peasant Viaud, and his
heirs for ever, everything that he had bought from
Count Pierre.

When Gabriel had finished reading, no one spoke
for a little while; it was so hard to realize the
crowning good fortune that had befallen them.
Peasant Viaud looked fairly dazed, and the mother
laughed and cried as she snatched Gabriel to her
and kissed him again and again. The younger
children did not understand what it all meant, and
so went on munching their sweetmeats without
paying much attention to the little piece of
parchment which Gabriel still held in his hand.

As for Gabriel, he really had had no idea that any
one could possibly be so happy as he himself was at
that moment! He had not the least notion of how it
had all come about; he only knew that his heart was

fairly bursting with gratitude to the dear God who had answered his little prayer so much more joyously and wonderfully than he had ever dared to dream of!

In his excitement he ran out of the house and hurried into the sheepfold, where he patted the soft woolly backs of each of the sheep, and then he raced around the snowy meadows trying to realize that all these belonged to his family for ever! And that Count Pierre could never again imprison his father or worry him with heavy taxes!

But the wonders of this wonderful day were not yet over; for presently, as Gabriel raised his eyes, he saw a strange horseman coming down the road and looking inquiringly in the direction of the Viaud cottage. Then seeing the boy standing in the meadow, the horseman called out:

"Ho, lad! Is this the farm of the peasant Viaud?"

"Yes, sir," answered Gabriel, coming up to the road; and then,

"Art thou Gabriel?" asked the rider, stopping and looking curiously at the little boy.

When again Gabriel wonderingly answered, "Yes, sir," the stranger dismounted, and, after tying his horse, began deliberately unfastening the two fat saddle-bags hanging over the back of the latter; and loading himself with as much as he could carry, he gave Gabriel an armful, too, and walked toward the cottage.

To the surprised looks and questions of Gabriel's father and mother, he only said that the Christ-child had been in the castle of the Lady Anne of Bretagne, and had ordered him to bring certain things to the family of a Norman peasant boy named Gabriel Viaud.

And such delightful things as they were! There was a great roll of thick, soft blue cloth, so that they could all be warmly clad without waiting for the mother to spin the wool from the sheeps' backs. There were nice little squirrel-fur caps for all the children; there were more yellow gold pieces; and then there was a large package of the most enchanting sweetmeats, such as the Bretons make at Christmas-time; little "magi-cakes," as they were called, each cut in the shape of a star and covered with spices and sugar; curious old-fashioned candies and sugared chestnuts; and a pretty basket filled with small round loaves of the fine, white bread of Bretagne; only instead of the ordinary baking, these loaves were of a special holiday kind, with raisins, and nuts, and dried sweet-locust blossoms sprinkled over the top.

Indeed, perhaps never before had so marvellous a feast been spread under a peasant roof in Normandy! All were beside themselves with delight; and while the younger children were dancing round and round in happy bewilderment, Gabriel snatched up a basket, and hurriedly filling it with some of the choicest of the sweetmeats, started off at a brisk run for the Abbey; for he wanted to share some of his Christmas happiness with Brother Stephen.

When he reached the Abbey, his eyes bright with excitement, and his cheeks rosy from the crisp cold air, and poured out to Brother Stephen the story of their fresh good fortune, the monk laughed with delight, and felt that he, too, was having the happiest Christmas he had ever known.

And then, by and by, when he took Gabriel by the hand and led him into the Abbey church for the beautiful Christmas service, as the little boy knelt on the stone floor and gazed around at the lovely garlands of green, and the twinkling candles and white Christmas roses on the altar, half-hidden by the clouds of fragrant incense that floated up from the censers the little acolytes were swinging to and fro,--as he listened to the glorious music from the choir, and above all, as he thought of how the dear God had answered his prayer, the tears sprang to his eyes from very joy and gratitude! And perhaps that Christmas morning no one in all France, not even King Louis himself, was quite so happy as the little peasant boy, Gabriel Viaud.

CHAPTER XI.

THE KING'S ILLUMINATOR

AND to say that he was happier than even King Louis, is saying a very great deal; for King Louis spent the day most delightfully in Bretagne, in the castle of his bride to be, the Lady Anne. And then, just after the holiday season had passed, early in

January, he and Lady Anne were married with great
ceremony and splendour.

After the wedding, for three months, the king and
queen lingered in Bretagne; enjoying themselves by
night with magnificent entertainments in the castle,
and by day in riding over the frosty fields and in
hunting, of which both of them were very fond. And
then in April, when the first hawthorn buds were
beginning to break, they journeyed down to Paris to
live in the king's palace.

Before long, King Louis and Queen Anne decided
to make a number of improvements in this palace;
and as they both were great lovers of beautiful
books, they determined, among other things, to
build a large writing-room where they could have
skilful illuminators always at work making lovely
books for them.

When this room was finished, and they began to
think of whom they would employ, the first one
they spoke of was Brother Stephen, whose exquisite
work on the book of hours had so delighted them.
But then, much as they wished to have him in the
palace, they did not think it possible to do so, as
they knew he belonged to the brotherhood of St.
Martin's Abbey, and so of course had taken vows to
spend his whole life there.

It chanced, however, soon after this, that King
Louis happened to have a little talk with the
messenger he had sent to the Abbey at Christmas
time to see about Gabriel. And this messenger told
the king that while there the Abbot, in speaking to

him of Brother Stephen's work, had said that the latter really wished to leave the brotherhood and go into the world to paint; and that, though he had refused his request to be freed from his vows, yet the monk had worked so faithfully at King Louis's book that he thought he had earned his freedom, and that perhaps he, the Abbot, had done wrong in forcing him to stay at the Abbey if he wished to study his art elsewhere.

In short, he had as much as said that if Brother Stephen ever again asked for his freedom, he would grant it; and this showed that the Abbot had relented and unbent a great deal more than any one could ever have believed possible.

When King Louis heard what the messenger told him, he was greatly pleased; and after talking it over with the queen, he decided to send the same messenger post-haste back to the Abbey to ask for the services of Brother Stephen before the Abbot might again change his mind.

Now King Louis was a very liberal monarch, and both he and Queen Anne liked nothing better than to encourage and help along real artists. And so they thought that they would supply Brother Stephen with money so that he could travel about and study and paint as he chose, even if he preferred always to paint larger pictures rather than to illuminate books; though they hoped that once in awhile he might spend a little time in their fine new writing-room.

When the messenger started, they told him to

explain all this to Brother Stephen, and let the latter plan his work in whatever way best pleased him.

But the queen gave particular orders that, if possible, the messenger was to bring the peasant boy, Gabriel Viaud, back to the palace with him; for she thought the lad's work on the page where he had written his little prayer showed such promise that she wished to see him, and to have him continue his training in the beautiful art of illumination.

The messenger, having thus received his orders, at once set out again for Normandy; and he found this second journey much more pleasant than the one he had made before, through the winter snows. For this time he rode under tall poplar-trees and between green hedgerows, where the cuckoos and fieldfares sang all day long. And when, after several days' travelling, he drew near St. Martin's Abbey, the country on either side of the road was pink with wild roses and meadowsweet, just as it had been a year before, when Gabriel used to gather the clusters of field-flowers for Brother Stephen to paint in the beautiful book.

Indeed, Gabriel still gathered the wild flowers every day, but only because he loved them; for though, since their better fortunes, he was again studying and working with Brother Stephen, the latter was then busy on a long book of monastery rules, with only here and there a coloured initial letter, and which altogether was not nearly so interesting as had been the book of hours with its lovely painted borders.

And so when the messenger reached the Abbey, and made known his errand, they were both overjoyed at the prospect King Louis offered them.

After talking with the messenger, the Abbot, true to his word, in a solemn ceremony, freed Brother Stephen from his vows of obedience to the rules of St. Martin's brotherhood; and then he gave both him and Gabriel his blessing.

Brother Stephen, who had been too proud to ask a second time for his freedom, was now delighted that it had all come about in the way it did, and that he could devote his time to painting anything he chose.

Gabriel, too, was enchanted at the thought of all that he could do and learn in the king's palace; and though he felt it hard to leave his home, Queen Anne had kindly made it easier for him by promising that sometimes he might come back for a little visit.

So in a few days he and Brother Stephen had made all their preparations to leave; and they set out, Gabriel going with the messenger directly to King Louis's palace in Paris; while Brother Stephen, taking the bag of gold pieces which the king and queen had sent for him, travelled to many of the great cities of Europe, where he studied the wonderful paintings of the world's most famous masters, and where he himself made many beautiful pictures. In this way he spent a number of happy months.

And then, just as a great many other people do, who

find out that as soon as they are not compelled to do a certain kind of work, they really like it very much better than they thought, so, Brother Stephen, being no longer obliged to illuminate books, all at once discovered that he really enjoyed painting them more than anything else in the world.

And so it was that, by and by, to the gratification of the king and queen, and above all to the great delight of Gabriel, he made his way to the great writing-room of the palace in Paris. And there, in the doing of his exquisite artistic work, he passed the rest of his long and happy life.

And through all the years the warm love and friendship between himself and Gabriel was as sweet and beautiful and as unchanging as any of the white and golden lilies that they painted in their rarest books. For Gabriel, too, became one of the finest illuminators of the time, and his work was much sought for by the great nobles of the land.

Indeed, to this day, many of the wonderful illuminations that were made in that writing-room are still carefully kept in the great libraries and museums of France and of Europe. And some time, if ever you have the happiness to visit one of these, and are there shown some of the painted books from the palace of King Louis XII. and Queen Anne, if the work is especially lovely, you may be quite certain that either Brother Stephen, or Gabriel, or perhaps both of them together, had a hand in its making.

Made in the USA
San Bernardino, CA
05 June 2016